LADYBIRD BOOKS

UK | USA | Canada | Ireland | Australia
India | New Zealand | South Africa

Puffin Books is part of the Penguin Random House group of companies
whose addresses can be found at global.penguinrandomhouse.com.

www.penguin.co.uk   www.puffin.co.uk   www.ladybird.co.uk

First published 2008
This edition published 2021
001

Copyright © Ladybird Books Ltd, 2008

The moral right of the author and illustrator has been asserted

The authorized representative in the EEA is Penguin Random House Ireland
Morrison Chambers, 32 Nassau Street, Dublin D02 YH68

A CIP catalogue record for this book is available from the British Library

ISBN: 978–0–723–29769–7

All correspondence to:
Ladybird Books, Penguin Random House Children's
One Embassy Garden's, 8 Viaduct Gardens, London SW11 7BW

Ladybird
Stories for 2 year olds

Written by Joan Stimson
Illustrated by Ingela Peterson

Christine's cornflakes

Christine was a very greedy hippo.
But she only liked one thing... cornflakes.

One morning Mum made a dreadful discovery.
There were no more cornflakes in the cupboard.
"I want my cornflakes!" yelled Christine. She banged
her spoon on the table.

Mum sent William to the shop. "Here's enough money for ten packets of cornflakes. You can take Dad's wheelbarrow."

The other hippos got on with their breakfast.

"Try some of my toast," said Toby.

"Don't want any," said Christine.
But then her tummy rumbled. So she tried
a small nibble of toast, then a bigger nibble.

"Try some of my apple," said Henry.

"Don't want any," said Christine.
But then her tummy rumbled. So she tried
a small bite of apple, then a bigger bite.

"Try some of my porridge," said Polly.

"Don't want any," said Christine. But then her tummy rumbled. So she tried a small spoonful. And then Christine spooned up the lot!

"Cornflakes!" called William.
He wheeled Dad's barrow into
the kitchen.

"Don't want any," said Christine.
She gave a little burp. "I'm too full... for cornflakes!"

11

The dirty dinosaur

"Just look at your knees, Douglas!"
cried Mrs Dinosaur.

"Brrrm, brrrm," said Douglas. He was much
too busy with his car to look at his knees.

"Have you seen your face, Douglas?"
asked Mr Dinosaur.

"Brrrm, brrrm," said Douglas. He was much too
busy driving his car to look in the mirror.

"Don't you ever take a bath?" sighed Granny Dinosaur.

"Brrrm, brrrm," said Douglas.
He never had time for a bath.

One day the dinosaurs went to town. On their way they passed a sign that said CAR WASH in big letters.

"Brrrm, brrrm," said Douglas. He couldn't wait to get inside. "Ooooh!" he cried. "It tickles... but I like it!"

"Come out of there, Douglas," cried Mum, Dad and Granny Dinosaur.

At last Douglas came out of the car wash.

"That was lovely!" he cried. And for the first time ever, Douglas was clean... all over.

The race

One day Farmer Brown went to market. While he was away, the farm animals decided to have a race.

Roger Ram jumped onto Farmer Brown's tractor. Bernie Bull jumped onto Mrs Brown's bike. Gary Goat jumped onto Billy Brown's skateboard.

16

"Hey! What about me?" clucked Hilary Hen.
But no one was listening.

"Ready," cried Roger.

"Steady," roared Bernie.

"Go!" yelled Gary. And they all rushed off together.

"Hey! Wait for me!" clucked Hilary. She jumped into Jenny Brown's trainers, which were far too big for her.

Roger was soon in front. But not for long.
Pop, splutter, pop! went the tractor.
It had run out of petrol.

Bernie sped past Roger.
But not for long. *Thump, thud, thump*! went
Mrs Brown's bike. Bernie was too heavy for a bike.
He'd squashed the tyres flat.

Gary overtook Roger and Bernie.
But not for long. *Wheeee... splash!*
went the skateboard.

Gary wasn't looking where he was
going. He landed in the pond.

"Hey!" clucked Hilary. She shuffled past Roger, Bernie and Gary. "I'm going to win!"

And that's just what she did.

Where's Teddy?

"Where's Teddy?" cried Brian
the elephant.
He couldn't find him anywhere.

"Have you seen Teddy?"
Brian asked the monkeys.

"Yes," said the monkeys.
"He came for a swing in the trees,
and we gave him a banana.
But he's gone now."

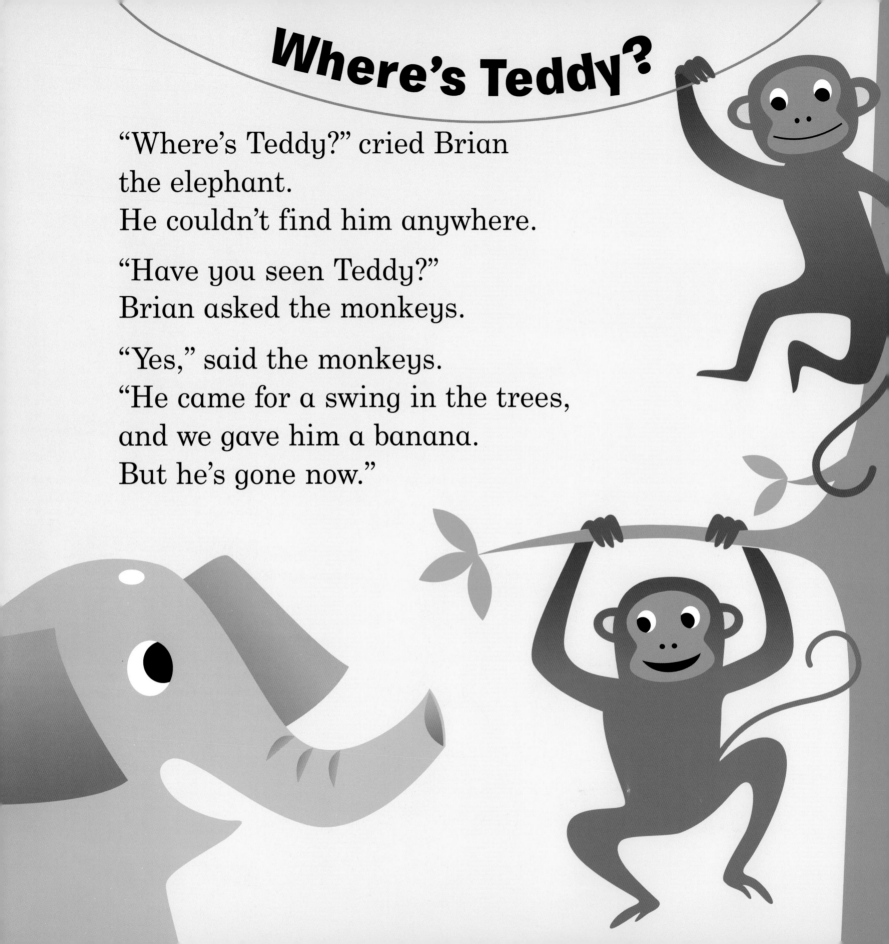

"Have you seen Teddy?" Brian asked the kangaroos.

"Yes," cried Jumper the kangaroo.
"He came for a ride in my pouch.
Up and down he went. But he's gone now."

"Have you seen Teddy?" Brian asked the polar bears.

"Yes," cried Roly Poly Bear. "He came for a swim on my back, and splashed all my friends. But he's gone now."

"Have you seen Teddy?" Brian asked the giraffes.

"Yes," said the giraffes. "We all had a game of hide and seek. But he's gone now."

"Have you seen Teddy?" Brian asked
Bert the zookeeper.

"Yes," said Bert. "He helped to eat up my tea.
But he's gone now."

Brian trudged home. It was getting late.
"I think I'll put on my pyjamas," he yawned.

Brian went into his bedroom.
And there, tucked up and
waiting for him was...

...Teddy!

Stop it!

"Stop it!" cried the tiger,
"I'm ticklish, can't you see?
I'm ticklish on my stripes.
I'm ticklish on my knee.

"Stop it!" cried the tiger,
"There's something I must do.
It's time for me to tickle —
For me to tickle you!"